A SLEEPING EIGHT

BY ROCHAK AGARWAL

Published by Notion Press
www.notionpress.com

ISBN: 9798895887165
9798895887196

Cover Design by Rochak Agarwal
Printed in India
First Edition: October 2024

ABOUT THE AUTHOR

Rochak Agarwal, a passionate storyteller from the vibrant city of Lucknow, India, believes in the magic of imagination. His journey into writing took an unexpected turn when his love for fiction sparked an idea that grew into 'A Sleeping Eight,' his debut novel. In this captivating tale, Rochak explores the beautiful complexities of love woven with mystery.

At the time of publishing this book, Rochak is 22 years old and balances a corporate job with his writing dreams. He finds inspiration in travelling, especially to the stunning mountains that fuel his creativity. A fan of sports and an avid reader, Rochak draws from a variety of experiences to bring his characters and stories to life.

Rochak's name, given by his grandfather, Late Radha Krishna Agarwal, means "interesting" in English—a perfect match for a writer who aims to captivate readers with every page. With 'A Sleeping Eight,' Rochak is thrilled to share his journey and invites you to dive into a world where love and mystery intertwine.

ABOUT THE BOOK

When Ethan Hart returns to Riverside, he finds himself stepping into a place both familiar and strange. Drawn back by memories of love, loss, and a life he left behind, he crosses paths with Sophie Monroe, a captivating musician whose presence reignites long-buried emotions. But what begins as a chance reunion soon unearths deeper mysteries—mysteries that neither of them are prepared to face.

As Ethan and Sophie reconnect, old wounds resurface, and the once peaceful town starts to feel like a maze of hidden truths and unexpected dangers. The more they try to find their way forward, the more tangled they become in a web of past choices and looming consequences.

A Sleeping Eight is a story of love, regret, and the powerful pull of the past. Suspenseful and emotionally gripping, it invites readers into a world where trust is delicate and every choice could change their lives. As Ethan and Sophie navigate the mysteries that bind them, they begin to realize that their connection may hold the key to a future they never imagined.

ACKNOWLEDGEMENTS

I would like to extend my heartfelt gratitude to my family and friends for their encouragement throughout this journey. Your support has meant the world to me and has been a source of motivation as I navigated the challenges of writing this book.

I would also like to express my appreciation to the many writers, storytellers, and creators whose work has inspired me along the way. Your words ignited my passion and encouraged me to explore the profound themes of love and loss in my own storytelling.

Additionally, I am thankful for the various resources and literature that shaped my writing process. The journey of crafting this story has been one of personal reflection and growth, and I cherish every moment spent bringing Sophie and Ethan's journey to life.

Finally, thank you to all the readers who are reading this book. Your support and engagement make all the effort worthwhile.

INDEX

Chapter One

ECHOES OF RIVERSIDE

Ethan Hart's return to Riverside was like stepping into a painting where past and present intertwined. The road ahead, familiar yet distant, unfurled like a bridge connecting him to memories he hadn't yet decided to confront. As his silver sedan glided through the early morning mist, each curve of the winding road seemed to pull him deeper into the heart of a place he had once called home.

Riverside was waking up, its streets still cradled in the gentle embrace of dawn. Ethan's gaze wandered over familiar sights—the quaint houses with manicured gardens, the old bookstore seemingly untouched by time, and the town square where he had spent countless hours as a child.

Before he left, Riverside had been a picture of simplicity. He could still recall the long summer days and high school memories. But behind those warm memories was a deeper pain—the family scandal that had torn his world apart and pushed him to leave, searching for a new life far from the town that held his past.

Ten years had passed since Ethan had last set foot in Riverside. In that time, his life had changed. He found success, made a name for himself, but his heart had never fully let go of the roots he left behind.

Now, as he parked his car near the old town square, a wave of nostalgia washed over him. It wasn't as lively as it used to be, with only a few people there, getting ready for the day ahead. The distant sound of pots and pans clanging in the café blended with the gentle calls of a vendor setting up his stall.

As Ethan stepped out of the car, he took a deep breath, allowing the familiar scents of fresh bread and coffee to ground him. The town was coming to life, and in a way, so was he. But, like Riverside, he knew things had changed—small, quiet shifts, both in the town and in himself. His footsteps echoed softly on the streets as he walked toward the square, his heart beating in sync with the quiet rhythm of the town.

The town square, once the heart of Ethan's youthful adventures, was now a mix of old memories and the present. The clock tower still stood tall in the center. The bookstore was still there, and the café where he and his friends had spent countless nights laughing and talking still filled the air with the familiar, inviting smell of fresh coffee.

As he wandered, the faint strumming of a guitar reached his ears. Ethan followed the sound and discovered a small crowd gathered around a musician setting up her performance. Sophie Monroe, with her dark hair pulled into a loose bun and wearing a flowing dress that seemed to mirror the spirit of the market itself, was tuning her guitar.

Her presence brought a burst of energy to the quiet square. She began to play with a natural grace, her fingers moving smoothly over the strings, creating music that was both calming and full of life. Ethan was immediately drawn to her performance, captivated by the rhythm and beauty of her melody.

Intrigued, Ethan decided to stay and listen. As Sophie played, he couldn't help but start humming along, his voice blending seamlessly with the melody. It wasn't long before Sophie noticed the stranger who seemed to have taken a keen interest in her music. She caught Ethan's eye, a playful spark lighting up her expression.

When the performance ended, Sophie put down her guitar and walked over to Ethan. "I didn't expect an audience today," she said with a smile. "You've got quite the voice. Ever thought about joining me on stage?"

Ethan, scratching his head. "I didn't mean to steal the spotlight. Just couldn't resist humming along. My parents were big into music, so it kind of runs in the family. They used to drag me to open mic nights when I was a kid."

Sophie's eyes widened with curiosity. "Really? That's impressive. So, do you have a hidden talent for singing or was that just a one-time thing?"

Ethan grinned. "Well, I suppose I can hold a tune or two. But I'm more of a 'casual performer' than a professional.

Sophie laughed, her eyes sparkling. "I can just picture it. Little Ethan on stage with his parents, belting out classic hits. It sounds adorable."

Ethan raised an eyebrow, playfully. "Adorable? Well, I must say, you've got quite the charm yourself. You turned an ordinary morning into a mini concert."

Sophie's cheeks flushed slightly, a touch of shyness blending with her confidence. "Thanks. I try to bring a bit of magic to Riverside with my music. It's my way of capturing the essence of the town."

Ethan picked up a flyer from a nearby stand where Sophie had begun to set up her promotional materials. "This flyer caught my eye. Are you performing here often?"

Sophie's eyes lit up as she began to explain. "Yes, I perform here every weekend. It's a way to connect with the community and share my love for music."

Ethan admired her dedication. "You've managed to capture more than just beauty. There's a whole story in your music."

Their conversation flowed effortlessly, each exchange revealing more about their lives and aspirations. Sophie spoke of her passion for music and her desire to keep the town's spirit alive through her work. Ethan shared snippets of his experiences in the city, though he kept the deeper, more painful parts of his past guarded.

As they talked, Ethan felt drawn to Sophie's warmth and sincerity. There was something magnetic about her, a spark that lit something inside him. He wondered if she felt it too, or if it was just the feeling of being back in a place that had once meant so much to him.

The market began to fill with more visitors, and the conversation between Ethan and Sophie took on a lighter, more flirtatious tone. Sophie playfully challenged Ethan to guess the meaning behind some of her song lyrics, her laughter ringing out like music in the busy market.

Ethan, catching the playful mood, decided to tease her a bit. "Alright, let's see if I can crack the code. What's the story behind your favourite song?"

Sophie's eyes sparkled with mischief. "Oh, that one's a secret. But I'll give you a hint: it's about chasing dreams and finding joy in the little things."

Ethan chuckled. "A song about dreams and joy. That's fitting, given you seem to bring both to the market."

Sophie laughed, shaking her head. "Flattery will get you everywhere, Mr. Hart. But I have to admit, you're not the worst guesser I've met."

Ethan leaned closer, his tone teasing. "Well, in that case, I'm going to guess that you're secretly a magical muse who inspires everyone around you."

Sophie's eyes widened in mock surprise. "Guilty as charged. But be careful, or I might just cast a spell that makes you sing a duet with me."

Ethan's grin widened. "A duet? That sounds amazing! I guess I'll need to start working on my harmonies. I wouldn't want to embarrass myself in front of Riverside's own music star.

Their banter was interrupted by a burst of laughter from a nearby vendor. Ethan noticed Sophie's smile fade slightly as her gaze shifted toward the edge of the square. He followed her glance and spotted a man in a dark coat, standing on the outskirts, watching Sophie with a strange, intense stare that sent a shiver down Ethan's spine, as if the air around them had suddenly grown heavy with unspoken tension.

Ethan's concern deepened. "Is everything alright? You seemed a bit distracted."

Sophie's smile returned, though it didn't quite reach her eyes. "Oh, it's nothing. Just some weird vibes today. You know how it is."

Ethan's worry grew. "If something's bothering you, maybe I can help."

Sophie's expression softened with gratitude, but she quickly dismissed his offer. "It's probably just me overthinking. But thanks for being so concerned."

As the market began to empty, Ethan noticed that Sophie's movements became more agitated. Her previous cheerfulness was replaced by a focused urgency. The man in the dark coat was still there, his gaze unwavering.

Ethan's protective instincts kicked in. "We need to get out of here. I'll help you pack up."

Sophie nodded, her anxiety clear. "Yes, please. I don't want to stick around and find out what that guy's up to."

They hurriedly packed up her stand, Ethan keeping a vigilant eye on the man who remained at the edge of the square. As they finished, Sophie glanced over her shoulder, her face pale with fear.

"We need to go," she whispered urgently. "He's coming closer."

Ethan grabbed her hand. "Follow me. We'll find a way out."

They moved quickly through the market, the once-bustling square now quiet. Ethan led Sophie towards a narrow alley, the walls closing in as they navigated the dimly lit passage.

Behind them, the faint sound of footsteps grew louder. Ethan's mind raced, trying to think of a way to escape. He spotted a fire escape ladder leading to the rooftop of a nearby building.

"We can climb up there," he said, pointing. "It might be our best chance."

Sophie's fear transformed into determination as they hurried up the fire escape, their hands gripping the cold metal rungs. The sound of footsteps below faded with each step they took, but the tension in the air lingered.

Finally reaching the rooftop, Ethan and Sophie paused to catch their breath. The city spread out beneath them, the rooftops glowing in the soft light of the setting sun.

Sophie sat down, "Thank you for saving me. I don't know what would have happened if you hadn't helped."

Ethan sat beside her, his own breath ragged. "I'm just glad we got out of there. But we need to figure out what's going on. That man—he was definitely up to something."

Sophie nodded, her eyes reflecting a mix of gratitude and concern. "I agree. We need to stay alert. But at least for now, we're safe."

Ethan looked at her, a teasing glint in his eyes. "You know, after all that excitement, I think we deserve a victory celebration. How about we find a nice café and celebrate our escape?"

Sophie's smile returned, her eyes twinkling. "A celebration sounds perfect. But only if you promise not to sing to me in the café."

Ethan grinned. "No promises. But I'll keep the performance to a minimum. Unless you're up for a duet, of course."

Sophie laughed, shaking her head. "You're impossible. But I suppose I could be convinced."

As the sun set, glowing golden over Riverside, Ethan and Sophie stayed on the rooftop, their bond growing stronger from the day's surprise adventure. The town's mysteries awaited them, and with their combined efforts, they were determined to uncover the truth behind the mysterious figure that had cast a shadow over their friendship.

Their journey was only beginning, but the echoes of Riverside seemed to promise more adventures—and perhaps a few more duets—awaiting them in the chapters to come.

Chapter Two

SHADOWS AND LIGHT

Sophie stood in the warm glow of the café, her heart still racing from the joy of reconnecting with Ethan. Their playful banter danced in the air, but beneath her smile, an uneasy feeling began to rise. The warmth of their laughter felt fragile, as if it could break at any moment.

As she glanced out the window, the lively streets of Riverside brought back memories of the life she had left behind—a life filled with both comforting and painful moments. With Ethan back in town, the shadows of her past seemed to stretch longer, reminding her that it was time to face what she had been trying to avoid for so long.

Sophie's gaze swept across the square, and for a fleeting moment, she thought she spotted a familiar figure in the distance. A man in a dark coat lingered at the edge of the café's entrance, his face hidden, but something about his posture felt unsettling. She quickly shook the thought away, focusing instead on the warmth of Ethan's presence.

Taking a deep breath, Sophie turned to Ethan, who looked at her with genuine curiosity. "Ethan," she began, her voice trembling slightly, "there's something important I need to share with you."

He leaned in closer, his gaze steady and encouraging. "What is it? You can tell me anything."

Sophie took a moment to steady her racing heart. Meeting Ethan's eyes made her feel safe, almost forgetting the fear that gripped her moments ago. Yet, she knew she couldn't keep this to herself any longer.

"It's about that man," she said, her voice shaky. "He's part of my past—a very painful past."

Ethan's interest grew, and he leaned in even closer. "What do you mean?"

Just as she was about to share more about her past, the café door swung open with a loud bang, letting in a gust of wind that sent napkins fluttering across the floor. The sudden noise jolted both of them, shattering the moment they had created. A lively group of students burst into the café, their laughter and chatter rising above the gentle hum of conversation, filling the air with a burst of energy.

Sophie's heart raced at the interruption, her thoughts suddenly tangled and unclear. She glanced over at Ethan, who looked just as taken aback. His expression shifted from curiosity to mild irritation, clearly frustrated by the distraction.

"Sorry, I—" she began, but the chance to open up faded along with the noise.

Ethan noticed the change in her expression, his brow furrowing with concern. "Sophie?"

She forced a smile, though it felt weak. "It's nothing. Just… it's complicated."

His eyes softened with understanding. "I get it. You don't have to talk about it if you're not ready."

After a moment, Ethan broke the silence, his eyes brightening with an idea. "How about we take a walk in the park? It might help clear our heads."

Looking into Ethan's reassuring gaze, Sophie felt a mix of gratitude and frustration. She wanted to share this part of herself with him, but the interruption had made it harder to find her voice.

Ethan tried to lighten the mood with playful banter. "So, what do you think of the park? Do you think it's romantic enough, or should we upgrade to a castle next time?"

Sophie laughed, the tension easing a little. "A castle? I'd say that's a bit too grand. Maybe just a nice coffee shop for our next date?"

"Deal. But only if you promise to keep me entertained with stories of your past adventures," he replied, grinning.

The gentle breeze rustled the trees as Ethan and Sophie continued their stroll through the park. Each step they took felt lighter, filled with laughter and shared secrets that seemed to dance in the air around them. As the sunlight filtered through the leaves, casting playful shadows on the ground, Ethan couldn't help but feel as if he had stepped into a dream.

"Do you believe in fate?" he asked, breaking the silence that had settled between them.

Sophie paused, her gaze drifting to the sky as if searching for the answer among the clouds. "I think we create our own fate, don't you? Every choice leads us to where we're meant to be."

Ethan nodded, captivated by her perspective. "So, me stumbling into you at the café was meant to happen?"

She chuckled softly, a melodic sound that sent a thrill through him. "Maybe. Or maybe it was just a happy coincidence."

"Either way, I'm glad it happened," he replied, his eyes sparkling with sincerity. "Today has been... incredible."

Ethan leaned against the railing, turning to face Sophie, who was now lost in thought, her brow slightly furrowed.

"What's on your mind?" he asked, concern creeping into his voice.

Sophie shook her head, as if shaking off the clouds of thought. "Just... memories. This place has a way of bringing them back."

Ethan's heart ached for her. "Good memories, I hope?"

She smiled softly, a hint of nostalgia in her eyes. "Some, yes. Others... not so much." She paused, biting her lip, as if debating whether to share more. "But I'm trying to focus on the good ones."

"Like today?" Ethan prompted, his heart racing as he took a step closer.

"Definitely," she said, her gaze meeting his, and in that moment, the world around them faded into a blur.

"Let's create some more," he suggested, his voice low and playful. "How about a dance? Right here, right now."

Sophie raised an eyebrow, a playful challenge flickering in her eyes. "A dance? Here? Are you sure we won't look ridiculous?"

"Absolutely not! We're creating our own moment," he replied, extending his hand, his heart pounding with anticipation.

With a hesitant grin, she placed her hand in his. He pulled her into a gentle twirl, their laughter echoing through the quiet park. The sunlight cast a warm glow around them, and for a moment, they were the only two people in the universe.

"Okay, I admit it," Sophie said between giggles, her cheeks flushed. "This is kind of fun."

"See? I told you!" Ethan exclaimed, feeling a surge of joy as he pulled her closer. "We should do this more often. It could be our thing."

"Only if it comes with a side of ice cream," she teased, leaning into him, their sides gently touching.

"Then it's settled. Dance, ice cream, and endless laughter," he replied, a grin stretching across his face.

As their laughter mixed with the sound of rustling leaves, Ethan noticed a change in the atmosphere. He leaned down, looking deeply into her eyes, his heart racing with a blend of excitement and vulnerability. "You know, I really enjoy this. I like you, Sophie."

The air between them felt electric, and Sophie's breath caught in her throat, her cheeks flushing with colour. "I like you too, Ethan. A lot," she confessed, her voice just above a whisper.

Ethan grinned, feeling excited. "Then maybe we should make this a regular thing. Just two friends exploring Riverside, making memories, and seeing where this goes."

"Only if you bring your dancing shoes next time," she replied, her eyes twinkling with mischief.

"Deal!" he said, their fingers interlacing as they began to walk back, the sun beginning to dip below the horizon.

"Maybe we should start a list of things to do together," Sophie suggested, her voice light and playful.

"Absolutely. I'll add ice cream, dancing, and maybe even karaoke," Ethan teased.

"Now you're talking!" Sophie laughed, and the sound filled him with warmth. "I'll have to warn you, though. I have the voice of an angel... or a very confused cat."

"I can't wait to hear it," he said, his heart swelling with affection for this girl who had unexpectedly woven her way into his life.

As they walked, they exchanged playful banter, their laughter weaving through the air like the vibrant colours of the sunset behind them. The world felt alive with possibilities.

Just as they were nearing the exit of the park, Ethan felt a rush of courage. "Sophie," he said, stopping her in her tracks. "Can I ask you something?"

"Of course! What is it?" she replied, her expression turning serious.

"If I were to ask you out on a proper date, would you say yes?" he asked, his heart pounding in his chest.

A moment of silence hung in the air, anticipation crackling between them. Sophie's eyes widened in surprise, then softened with warmth. "Yes, Ethan, I would love that."

Ethan felt a grin stretch across his face, a rush of excitement filling him. "Then it's a date!"

As they left the park, the world felt alive with possibilities, and with every step, he could feel the promise of something beautiful blossoming between them.

Chapter Three

THE BRIDGE BETWEEN LOVE AND LOSS

The days that followed were filled with a delightful mix of laughter and shared moments between Ethan and Sophie. Their connection deepened like the roots of ancient trees, intertwining in a way that felt both natural and unavoidable. They spent afternoons exploring Riverside, hand in hand, uncovering hidden cafes and secret spots that seemed to be meant just for them. Each moment spent together felt like a melody—rich and harmonious, wrapping around them like a warm embrace.

The rooftop of the Riverside bookshop had become their special place. It was quiet, tucked away from the hustle and bustle of the town below, offering a perfect view of the sun setting over the hills. But today, despite the golden glow of the sunset and the gentle breeze, Ethan couldn't enjoy it as he usually did. An unspoken tension hung in the air, heavy and noticeable, and he knew it was connected to the man Sophie had mentioned.

He didn't know much about him yet—just that he was a part of Sophie's past, and judging by the way she reacted when she saw him earlier that day, he wasn't the kind of guy you just forget about. Ethan leaned forward, glancing at Sophie, who had pulled her knees to her chest, staring out at the horizon as if it could offer some kind of answer.

He couldn't stand the tension anymore.

"So…" Ethan began, breaking the silence, "Are we going to talk about it, or should we just pretend like everything's totally normal?"

Sophie's head turned slowly, her lips tugging into a small, tired smile. "You don't really do the whole 'ignoring things' approach, do you?"

"Not really my style," Ethan replied, grinning slightly. "I'm more of a 'let's deal with it head-on' kind of guy."

Sophie sighed, resting her chin on her knees. "I figured."

For a moment, she just sat there, looking at him. Ethan could tell she was trying to decide how much to say. Her eyes held a mix of fear and weariness, but also something else—trust. That gave him hope.

She shifted slightly, stretching out her legs as if preparing herself for a long conversation. "I guess I owe you an explanation," Sophie started softly, her voice quieter than usual. "But it's not an easy story."

Ethan nodded, leaning in, giving her his full attention. "I'm not going anywhere, Sophie. Take your time."

Sophie took a deep breath, looking down at her hands for a moment before she began. "His name is Paul. We met a few years ago, when I was… in a different place. He was charming—no, scratch that—he was perfect, at least in the beginning. The kind of guy that walks into a room and just draws everyone in. I fell for him, hard and fast. But, like most too-good-to-be-true stories, things started to change."

Her voice grew a bit quieter as she continued, the words seeming to carry more weight with every sentence. "At first, I didn't see the warning signs. He seemed protective, but it quickly turned into something dark. He would read my messages and accuse me of lying if I didn't show him everything. He claimed it was for my safety, insisting that only he could truly look out for me. What I thought was love soon felt more like a prison.

He isolated me from everyone who cared about me, planting seeds of doubt about their intentions. 'Your friends are only pretending to be nice; they don't really care about you like I do,' he would say. Gradually, I began to believe him, cutting ties with friends and family until I was completely dependent on him. When I wanted to see anyone, he would explode with anger, accusing me of abandoning him. One night, I tried to attend a family gathering, and he physically blocked the door, demanding I choose between him and my family."

Ethan's jaw tightened, but he kept quiet, letting her continue.

"The worst part was the fear, I had to be very careful. If I made even a small mistake, he would lash out verbally, calling me stupid or incompetent and making me feel like I was the cause of all his problems. Living with him was like being in a storm; I had to constantly adapt to avoid his rage. I remember one time I forgot to text him that I was running late. He didn't just get mad; he turned it into a massive fight, claiming I was disrespecting him and threatening to leave if I didn't change. In that chaos, I lost myself, convinced I was the problem. By the end, I wasn't just lost—I was terrified of what he might do if I ever tried to break free. I knew I had to escape, but it felt impossible."

Ethan clenched his fists, anger simmering just beneath the surface. He hated this Paul guy already, and he hadn't even met him.

"I tried to leave once," Sophie said, her voice barely above a whisper now. "That's when things got scary. He showed up at my apartment, furious, said I couldn't just walk away from him. He didn't hit me, but the way he looked at me, the way he made me feel like I belonged to him... I was terrified. I packed up everything I could carry, changed my number, and tried to disappear."

Ethan was quiet for a moment, processing everything she'd said. He felt a mix of emotions—anger, frustration, sadness—but more than anything, he felt protective. He reached out and gently placed a hand on hers.

"Why didn't you tell me this sooner?" he asked softly, his eyes locked on hers.

Sophie let out a soft laugh, though there was no humour in it. "Because I didn't want you to think I was some damaged girl with baggage. I wanted to be the fun, carefree version of myself that I used to be. The version of me before Paul."

Ethan shook his head. "You're not damaged, Sophie. You're strong—stronger than you think."

Sophie smiled, but it was tinged with sadness. "I don't feel strong."

"Well, you are. Trust me, I've known you long enough to say that with confidence," Ethan replied, squeezing her hand gently. "And besides, you're talking to a guy who once got locked out of his own apartment because he forgot his keys and his phone inside. If anyone's damaged, it's me."

Sophie laughed, a genuine laugh this time, and Ethan couldn't help but smile back.

"You're ridiculous," she said, shaking her head in amusement.

"I prefer the term 'charmingly flawed,' but I guess ridiculous works too," Ethan replied with a grin. "And for the record, I'm not going anywhere. You're stuck with me."

Sophie's smile softened, and for the first time since they had started discussing Paul, she seemed to relax a bit. "You really don't scare easily, do you?"

"Not when it comes to you," Ethan said, his tone light but sincere. "Besides, I think I'd be more scared of you than some guy with control issues."

Sophie raised an eyebrow, a playful smirk appearing on her lips. "Oh? Is that so?"

"Absolutely. You've mastered that 'don't mess with me' look," Ethan teased, leaning back against the rooftop edge. "One glare from you, and even Paul would probably back off."

Sophie shook her head, her smile still lingering. "I wish that were true."

Ethan tilted his head, studying her for a moment. "He's still bothering you, isn't he? Paul, I mean."

Sophie hesitated, "I don't know," she admitted. "I hadn't seen or heard from him in a while, but today, seeing him in the market... It was like a punch to the gut. I didn't think he'd find me again, but he always does."

Ethan frowned. "And what does he want? Does he think he can just walk back into your life?"

Sophie shrugged, her expression a mix of frustration and helplessness. "I don't know. He's the kind of person who doesn't like losing control. I think he just wants to remind me that I can't escape him—that no matter where I go, he'll always be lurking."

"That's not going to happen," Ethan said firmly. "You're not alone in this anymore. If he tries to come near you again, we'll handle it together."

Sophie glanced at him, her eyes searching his face. "You say that like it's easy. But you don't know what he's capable of, Ethan. He's connected, in ways you wouldn't believe."

"Let me guess—he's got a secret underground network of spies, right?" Ethan joked, trying to lighten the mood.

Sophie rolled her eyes, but her smile returned, if only for a moment. "I'm serious."

"So am I," Ethan said, his tone softening again. "Look, I know you're scared, and I get why. But I'm not going to let him hurt you. And I'm definitely not letting him scare me off."

"You're crazy, you know that?" Sophie muttered, though there was warmth in her voice.

"Yeah, but I'm your kind of crazy," Ethan replied, giving her a crooked grin.

Sophie shook her head, laughing softly. "That you are."

They sat in silence for a while, the soft hum of the evening filling the air around them. The sun had dipped below the horizon now, casting long shadows over the town. Despite the darkness creeping in, Ethan felt lighter, knowing Sophie had trusted him enough to share her story.

"I'm serious about this, Sophie," Ethan said after a moment. "You don't have to face him alone. If Paul comes back, we'll deal with him. You're not running anymore."

Sophie's expression softened as she looked at him. "Thank you," she whispered, her voice full of emotion.

"Anytime," Ethan replied, his voice gentle but sure. "Now, let's get off this rooftop before I freeze. I'm already starting to lose feeling in my toes."

Sophie laughed again, standing up and brushing off her jeans. "I told you to bring a jacket, but no, Mr. 'I'm fine' doesn't need one."

"Hey, I'm trying to keep up my tough-guy image here. Can't ruin that with a jacket," Ethan shot back, giving her a playful push as they made their way to the ladder.

Once they were back on the street, walking next to each other, Sophie quietly slipped her hand into his. Ethan looked down at her, surprised but happy. They walked together in comfortable silence, the cool night air surrounding them as they made their way to her place.

"You know," Ethan said, breaking the quiet, "If you really wanted to scare Paul off, you could always tell him you're dating me. That ought to do the trick."

Sophie raised an eyebrow, a smile playing at her lips. "Oh? And why's that?"

Ethan puffed out his chest, walking with exaggerated confidence. "Because I'm a terrifying force of nature, obviously."

Sophie snorted, shaking her head. "Right. I'll be sure to keep that in mind."

They walked a little further before Sophie spoke again, her voice quieter this time. "Thank you, Ethan. For… everything. I didn't think I'd ever find someone who'd be willing to stick around, knowing all this."

Ethan smiled, squeezing her hand. "Like I said, you're stuck with me."

Sophie glanced up at him, her expression soft and full of gratitude. "I'm starting to think that might not be such a bad thing."

As they neared her apartment building, Ethan slowed his pace, turning to face her. The streetlights above cast a soft glow on Sophie's face, highlighting the worry lines that had formed during their conversation. He stopped, looking down at her seriously.

"I mean it, Sophie. I'm not going anywhere. We're in this together."

Sophie nodded slowly, her eyes shimmering with something Ethan couldn't quite place. "I know," she whispered.

And in that moment, something shifted between them. The weight of Sophie's past hadn't disappeared, but it felt lighter now, as if she didn't have to carry it all on her own anymore.

As they walked the last few steps to her door, Ethan couldn't shake the feeling that this was just the beginning of something bigger. Paul might have been part of Sophie's past, but if he showed up again, Ethan was ready.

They stood in front of her building for a moment, neither of them wanting to end the night just yet.

"See you tomorrow?" Ethan asked, his voice hopeful.

Sophie smiled, a soft, genuine smile. "Yeah. Tomorrow."

And for the first time in a long time, tomorrow didn't seem so uncertain.

Chapter Four

THE WEIGHT OF SILENCE

Sophie, was set to perform at a local venue today. It was meant to be a celebration of her artistry and passion. Ethan sat in the small, dimly lit room, his heart thudding with anticipation and anxiety. Today was supposed to be a celebration, and he had promised to be there, cheering her on as she showed off her talent. Yet, with every passing minute without a message or call from Sophie, a rising sense of unease settled in the pit of his stomach. He looked at his phone for what felt like the hundredth time, hoping for a notification that never arrived.

The vibrant buzz of the crowd echoed in his mind, making him ache for her even more. He could picture her on stage, her eyes sparkling as she poured her soul into her music. But today felt different. An invisible barrier separated him from her world, and he couldn't shake the feeling that something was off.

Finally, he couldn't stand the waiting any longer. He decided to head to the venue, hoping to see her after the show. The night was cool, and the streets buzzed with excitement, laughter, and music, but all he felt was a heavy weight on his chest. As he got closer to the venue, the sound of cheering welcomed him. The crowd erupted as Sophie stepped onto the stage, and Ethan's heart swelled with pride as he slipped inside, weaving through the excited audience, all eager to see her perform.

Under the bright lights, Sophie radiated confidence, capturing everyone's attention. When she began to sing, her voice filled the room like a soft, soothing breeze. But as the song went on, he couldn't shake the feeling that something was wrong. Sophie's eyes, which usually sparkled with passion, looked distant. She smiled, but the warmth didn't quite reach her gaze.

Ethan's phone buzzed in his pocket just as the last note of Sophie's song echoed through the venue. He pulled it out, expecting a text from her, but his heart sank when he saw an unfamiliar number. The message was simple: "You don't know what you're getting into. Stay away from her."

Before he could process the message, his phone buzzed again. Another message from the same unknown number. This time, it was a photo of Sophie at the concert, her face illuminated by the stage lights, a look of joy on her face. But the timestamp showed it had been taken just two minutes ago. A cold shiver ran down Ethan's spine.

Panic surged through him as he scanned the crowd, his heart racing. The weight of the message settled heavily in his stomach. Paul was watching. Who else could it be? The thought made Ethan's blood run cold. He felt the urgency of the situation clawing at him. He had to protect her.

The performance came to an end, and the applause was deafening. Ethan clapped along with the crowd, but his heart raced with confusion. He pushed his way toward the stage. He needed to find Sophie, to shield her from whatever threat loomed nearby.

However, when he reached the front, he found only emptiness. The stage crew was packing up, but Sophie was nowhere to be found. Panic surged through him, his heart pounding as he approached one of the staff members. "Where's Sophie?" he asked, his voice strained.

"She just left," the crew member replied, not meeting his eyes. "She was in a hurry."

"Left? What do you mean?" His voice rose, the worry twisting into frustration.

"Look, man, I don't know. She was great tonight, but she didn't say where she was going," the staff member shrugged, his indifference cutting deeper than Ethan expected.

Ethan's mind raced. Why would she leave without telling him? Was something wrong? Was Paul already involved? He couldn't shake the urgency that clawed at him. His hands trembled slightly as he pulled out his phone, ready to call her again.

He pressed the call button, and the phone rang. No answer. Each ring deepened his sense of dread. It was as if the universe was conspiring against him. Ethan felt a growing sense of frustration and helplessness. He hated feeling this way, especially when he couldn't protect her.

Fueled by the rising tension inside him, Ethan hurried outside, scanning the dimly lit streets. He needed to find Sophie. Pushing his way through the crowd of concertgoers, his heart raced with every unanswered call he made to her phone.

As he stepped onto the street, his breath caught in his throat when he spotted a dark car parked nearby. Something about it felt off. Instinct kicked in, and a familiar sense of recognition hit him. Was that Paul's car? Ethan's heart pounded harder as he moved closer, a knot of fear tightening in his chest.

Then he saw her. Sophie stepped out of the venue, her face brightening as she laughed with a friend, completely unaware of the danger nearby. For a moment, relief washed over him, but it quickly vanished when he noticed the man leaning against the car. He seemed relaxed, but his presence felt threatening. It was Paul.

Ethan's blood ran cold as he watched Paul's gaze fixate on Sophie, his smile twisting into something darker. Just then, Sophie's laughter faltered, and her smile faded as she noticed Paul. Ethan's heart sank as he watched the scene unfold in what felt like slow motion.

Paul moved toward her, and before Ethan could react, he reached out and grabbed her arm. "Hey, Sophie. We need to talk," he said, his voice smooth but laced with menace.

Sophie recoiled, clearly uncomfortable. "Let go of me, Paul! I don't want to talk to you."

But Paul tightened his grip, pulling her closer, and Ethan felt a surge of adrenaline. This wasn't just a conversation; this was a confrontation.

"Hey!" Ethan shouted, stepping forward, his voice breaking through the night. "Let her go!"

Paul turned, surprise flashing across his face before a smirk replaced it. "And who are you? Her knight in shining armour?"

Ethan didn't reply. Instead, he rushed forward, a mix of fear and anger driving him to confront Paul. But just as he reached them, Paul shoved Sophie toward the car, forcing her into the back seat.

"No!" Ethan shouted, running after them. Adrenaline rushed through him as he reached the car just in time to see Paul climb into the driver's seat.

"Get out of the car!" Ethan yelled, banging his hands against the window. Inside, Sophie's eyes were wide with fear, and it sent a wave of panic through him.

Paul smirked again, his eyes gleaming with evil. "You should have stayed away, Ethan. This isn't your fight."

Ethan didn't hesitate. He pulled the car door open, surprising Paul. A struggle began as Paul lunged at him, and they fell to the ground. The world around them turned chaotic, and the sounds of the city faded into the background as the fight unfolded.

Ethan's heart raced as he fought with Paul, trying to take control. Every punch thrown felt like a fight for Sophie's safety. He could hear her muffled cries from inside the car, urging him to fight harder, to protect her.

"Let her go!" Ethan grunted, pushing Paul away and quickly getting back on his feet. He took a moment to catch his breath, adrenaline surging through him.

Paul stood, brushing himself off, his expression darkening. "You think you can take me on? You have no idea what you're dealing with."

Ethan clenched his fists, frustration bubbling up. "So what? You're just going to let her suffer?"

Paul laughed, but there was no humour in it. "You think you can save her? You're not even in the same league."

With that, Paul charged at Ethan, but Ethan stood his ground, prepared for the attack. He dodged the first blow, pivoting to deliver a powerful kick that struck Paul's side, sending him stumbling back.

Ethan didn't hesitate; he followed up with a punch to Paul's jaw, the impact reverberating through his body. Paul staggered but quickly regained his composure, determination igniting in his eyes.

As they exchanged blows, the fight intensified. Ethan could feel the weight of every moment. This was more than just a physical battle; it was a fight for Sophie's freedom. He could hear her shouting his name, urging him on, and it fueled his resolve.

With one final surge of energy, Ethan tackled Paul, pinning him to the ground. "You're done!" he shouted, his voice filled with raw emotion. Paul struggled beneath him, but Ethan held firm, refusing to let go.

"Get off me!" Paul growled, but Ethan stood firm. He needed to ensure Sophie was safe. With a sudden rush of adrenaline, Ethan knocked Paul's arm away and quickly got back on his feet. Paul lay there, breathless and beaten.

"Let's go!" Ethan shouted as he hurried back to Sophie. He reached for her, pulling her into his arms. "I'm so sorry. I thought I lost you."

Sophie hugged him tightly, her body trembling. "I was so scared. I didn't know what he was going to do."

"We need to get out of here," Ethan said, glancing back at Paul, who was still on the ground, his anger simmering just beneath the surface.

"Can you drive?" Ethan asked, urgency flooding his voice.

"I... I think so," she stammered, her eyes darting to the side as if she could still see Paul, waiting for the right moment to strike.

Ethan quickly took the driver's seat, his heart racing. He glanced at Sophie, who was visibly shaken, but her determination shone through. "Just stay close to me. We'll get out of here."

As he started the engine, Sophie reached over, her hand shaking as it rested on his arm. "Ethan, he's going to come after us. He won't let this go."

"I know," Ethan replied, his jaw tightening. "But we can't let fear control us. I won't let him hurt you again."

He turned the car onto the main road, weaving through the streets as his mind raced with plans and possibilities. They needed a safe place—somewhere to regroup and figure out what to do next. The weight of the night's events hung heavily in the air, a palpable reminder of the danger they were facing.

"Where should we go?" Sophie asked, her voice barely above a whisper.

"Let's head to my place. It's not far, and we can talk there," Ethan said, trying to keep his tone steady despite the anxiety churning inside him.

Sophie nodded, but Ethan could see the fear in her eyes. He glanced in the rearview mirror, half-expecting to see Paul's car following them. But the street behind was empty. For now, they were safe.

As they reached Ethan's apartment, he parked quickly, glancing around as they stepped out of the car. The air was thick with tension, and every sound made them both jump. "Stay close," Ethan instructed, leading her to the entrance.

Once inside, he locked the door behind them, the click echoing in the silence. Ethan turned to Sophie, who was still visibly shaken. He wanted to comfort her, to tell her everything would be okay, but he couldn't shake the fear that loomed over them.

"Let's sit down," he said, guiding her to the small living room. He switched on a lamp, "You're safe here."

Sophie took a deep breath, looking around as if trying to ground herself in the moment. "Ethan, I didn't think he'd come after me like that. I thought I was free from him."

Ethan's heart ached for her. "You are free. You just need to stay strong. We'll figure this out together." He took her hands in his, feeling the warmth of her skin against his. "I'm not letting him take you away from me."

Sophie's gaze softened, but the shadows of fear still lingered in her eyes. "What if he comes back? What if he tries to hurt you next?"

Ethan's resolve strengthened at her words. "I won't let that happen. I'm going to do whatever it takes to keep you safe." He could feel the weight of the promise he was making, and he meant every word.

"I don't want you to get hurt because of me," Sophie said, her voice trembling.

He shook his head, pulling her closer. "You mean everything to me, Sophie. I can't just sit back and let someone hurt you. We'll find a way to stop him."

Suddenly, a loud bang jolted them both, and Ethan's heart skipped a beat. He turned toward the window, peering out into the night. "Did you hear that?" he whispered, a knot tightening in his stomach.

Sophie nodded, her eyes wide with fear. "What was that?"

"I don't know," Ethan replied, moving cautiously toward the window. He peered through the blinds, scanning the street below. Everything seemed calm, but he couldn't shake the feeling that they were being watched.

"Ethan!" Sophie's voice pulled him back to reality, and he quickly closed the door, his heart racing. "What's happening?"

"Paul's here," Ethan said, his voice barely above a whisper. "I think he's waiting for us."

Sophie gasped, her hand flying to her mouth. "What do we do?"

Ethan turned back to her, the urgency of the situation igniting a fire within him. "We need to call the police. This isn't just a threat anymore; he's right outside."

Sophie nodded, fear etched on her face. Ethan grabbed his phone, but just as he dialed, another loud bang reverberated through the apartment, making both of them jump.

"Get back!" Ethan shouted, shoving Sophie behind him as he pressed the call button. His pulse quickened, and he felt the adrenaline coursing through his veins.

Before the call connected, a voice rang out from outside. "Sophie! I know you're in there!"

Ethan's breath caught in his throat. It was Paul. "We have to go! Now!" He grabbed Sophie's hand, pulling her toward the back exit of his apartment.

As they moved, Ethan's mind raced with possibilities. He knew Paul wouldn't give up easily, and they needed a plan. If they could make it to the alley behind the building, they might have a chance to escape unnoticed.

"Ethan, what are we going to do?" Sophie's voice trembled.

"Just trust me," he replied, determination fueling his every move. They reached the back door, and Ethan hesitated for just a moment.

He opened the door slowly, peering into the dark alley. "Okay, on three," he whispered. "One, two... three!"

They burst through the door and into the alley, hearts racing as they dashed away from the apartment. Ethan glanced back, half-expecting to see Paul right behind them. The darkness enveloped them, but they pressed on, adrenaline pushing them forward.

"Where do we go?" Sophie gasped, trying to keep up with his hurried pace.

"Just keep running!" Ethan urged, his mind racing. He had to find a place to hide, somewhere Paul couldn't reach them. They turned a corner, and Ethan spotted an old, abandoned storage facility a few blocks down.

"Over there!" he shouted, pointing toward the building. They raced toward it, their hearts racing in their chests.

When they reached the door, Ethan quickly swung it open, guiding Sophie inside. "Hurry!" he urged, shutting the door behind them. They were surrounded by darkness, and the faint smell of dust filled the air.

"Do you think he saw us?" Sophie asked, her voice trembling.

"I don't know, but we can't stay here for long," Ethan replied, glancing around. "Let's see if there's a way out in the back."

As they moved further into the storage facility, Ethan's heart raced faster. The shadows around them seemed to shift and move, heightening his anxiety. The silence felt heavy, and he could almost hear his heartbeat echoing in the quiet.

Suddenly, they heard it—a faint noise from outside, the unmistakable sound of an engine getting closer. A wave of dread washed over Ethan. Paul was still out there, and they needed to act fast.

"Ethan," Sophie whispered, her eyes wide with fear. "What if he finds us?"

"We won't let that happen," Ethan said, his voice firm. "We need to find another exit."

They moved cautiously through the building, and Ethan's mind raced with thoughts of what they could do next—how to confront Paul without putting Sophie in danger again.

Just then, a loud crash echoed from the front of the building. Ethan froze, heart pounding. "He's here!"

They quickly hid behind a stack of crates, breathing fast and quietly. Ethan peeked out from behind the crates and saw Paul walking into the facility, his eyes searching the shadows and a dangerous grin on his face.

"Come out, come out, wherever you are," Paul taunted, his voice dripping with malice. "I just want to talk."

Ethan felt Sophie's hand grip his tightly, and he turned to her, his eyes meeting hers. "We need to distract him," he whispered urgently.

"What? How?" she replied, fear evident in her tone.

Ethan thought for a moment. "I'll create a diversion. When he goes for it, you run. Find a way to get help."

Sophie shook her head strongly. "No! I won't leave you!"

"I can't let him take you again," Ethan insisted. "You have to trust me."

The air was thick with tension, pressing down on them, but there was no time to waste. Ethan took a deep breath, preparing himself for what was to come. He scanned the area and noticed an old metal pipe lying on the ground nearby. It would have to do.

"Just stay hidden and be ready," he instructed, his voice steady. He slowly stepped out from behind the crates, gripping the pipe tightly in his hands as he stepped into the dim light.

"Paul!" Ethan shouted, his voice echoing off the walls. "Over here!"

Paul turned sharply, surprise flashing across his face before it morphed into a smirk. "Ethan! I was wondering when you'd show up."

Ethan took a step back, keeping his distance. "Stay away from her!"

"Oh, Ethan, you're making this so much harder than it needs to be," Paul replied, his tone mocking. "Just let her go, and I'll forget this ever happened."

Ethan didn't respond. He charged at Paul, launching the pipe with all his strength, connecting with Paul's side. The blow sent Paul staggering back, but he quickly regained his footing.

The fight escalated as they exchanged blows, the intensity of their struggle echoing through the dimly lit storage facility. Every punch Ethan threw felt like a testament to his determination to protect Sophie, and he could feel his adrenaline surging. Paul fought back fiercely, his eyes shining with a threatening look as he countered every move.

"Is this really how you want to play this, Ethan?" Paul sneered, dodging another of Ethan's strikes. "You're only making things worse for yourself and for her."

Ethan's heart raced, his mind spinning. I can't let him win. I have to keep Sophie safe. With renewed focus, he swung the pipe again, this time catching Paul off guard. The metal connected with Paul's shoulder, and he stumbled backward, cursing under his breath.

"Get away from her!" Ethan shouted, a primal roar erupting from his throat as he pressed his advantage, feeling a surge of hope. He had to finish this.

Just as Ethan was about to launch another attack, Paul's foot caught his ankle, sending him crashing to the ground. Pain shot through his body, and for a moment, everything went dark as the world tilted around him.

Sophie's panicked voice broke through the fog. "Ethan!"

Ethan pushed himself up, shaking his head to clear the dizziness. He saw Paul moving closer, a predatory smile spreading across his face. "You really thought you could protect her? You're pathetic!"

Ethan gritted his teeth, adrenaline surging through him again as he scrambled to his feet. "I won't let you hurt her!"

With fierce determination, he lunged at Paul, who was briefly caught off guard. The two men grappled fiercely, exchanging blows, but Ethan's resolve remained strong. He could hear Sophie's muffled cries, urging him to fight harder.

Suddenly, an idea struck Ethan as he noticed the stack of crates nearby. He pushed Paul away and, with a surge of strength, knocked one of the crates toward him. Paul barely managed to dodge it, but that brief distraction was all Ethan needed.

Ethan seized the opportunity and swung the pipe again with all his might. This time, it struck Paul squarely on the head, and he crumpled to the ground, dazed and defeated.

"Now," Ethan panted, rushing back to Sophie, who was watching wide-eyed. "Let's get out of here."

They fled through the back exit of the storage facility, the adrenaline still pumping through their veins. Ethan kept his hand clasped firmly around Sophie's as they dashed into the alley, breathing heavily.

"What now?" Sophie asked, her voice shaky but determined. "What if he gets up?"

"He won't follow us right away," Ethan replied, glancing back at the facility. "We have to get to my apartment. It's the safest place for now."

Sophie nodded, and they kept running, the fear of being caught pushing them on. When they reached the street, Ethan's heart raced—not just from the effort of running, but from the worry that Paul could show up at any time.

Once they reached Ethan's apartment, he quickly guided Sophie inside and locked the door behind them. The silence felt heavy, a stark contrast to the chaos outside. Ethan leaned against the door, closing his eyes for a brief moment, letting the weight of the night settle on his shoulders.

"Ethan?" Sophie's voice broke through his thoughts, tinged with worry.

He opened his eyes and turned to her, seeing the fear still etched on her face. "We're safe now," he assured her, trying to muster a comforting smile. "For now, at least."

"Did you really think he wouldn't come after us again?" Sophie said, her voice trembling. "He's dangerous."

Ethan nodded, his heart heavy. "I know. And we need to report this to the police, but right now, I just want to make sure you're okay."

Sophie stepped closer, her eyes searching his. "What if he finds out we went to the police?"

"Then we'll be ready," Ethan promised, taking her hands in his. "I won't let him take you away from me again. We'll figure this out together."

As they sat in the dim light of the living room, the weight of the world felt a little lighter. They were safe for the moment, and in the midst of the chaos, a glimmer of hope flickered between them. They were united, ready to face whatever came next, together.

"I'm not going to let fear control us," Ethan said, squeezing her hands. "We'll plan our next move, and we'll be ready for him. Together."

Sophie nodded, the resolve returning to her eyes. "Together."

And in that moment, as they faced the uncertainty ahead, they both knew that their bond had only grown stronger through the darkness.

Chapter Five

TORN APART

The sun dipped below the horizon, casting long shadows across the living room as Ethan stood protectively in front of Sophie. The tension between them was strong, charged with the unspoken fears that had grown ever since Paul's threatening return. Sophie sat curled up on the couch, a blanket wrapped tightly around her shoulders, her eyes darting toward the window as if expecting Paul to appear at any moment.

"Ethan," she said finally, her voice barely above a whisper, breaking the heavy silence. "We need to talk about Paul."

He felt a surge of protectiveness, instinctively shifting closer to her. "I know we do. But let's not focus on him right now. We just escaped him. We're safe here."

Sophie looked away, her gaze lost in the flickering shadows that danced across the walls. "Safe? I don't feel safe, Ethan. He's out there. I can't shake the feeling that he's watching us."

Ethan stepped closer, urgency propelling him forward. "We can't let him get to us. We've faced threats before, and we've made it through. What makes this time different?"

"Because he's more dangerous now," she replied, her voice trembling as fear seeped through her resolve. "He's not just a shadow anymore; he's a predator, and I'm terrified of what he'll do to you if he finds out we're together."

Ethan's heart raced at her words. He had always known Paul was a threat, but hearing Sophie voice her fears made the reality sink in deeper. "I don't care about the risk," he insisted. "I'm not going to let him control us. You mean too much to me."

"But you don't understand!" Sophie shot back, panic creeping into her voice. "Every time I think about what he could do... it terrifies me. He's already shown us how far he'll go."

Just then, a loud knock shattered the fragile calm. Both of them froze, and Ethan's heart raced. "Stay back," he ordered, inching toward the door. "I'll handle this."

"Ethan—" she started, but he held up a hand, focusing on the looming threat outside.

He opened the door, and there stood Paul, a menacing grin plastered across his face, the flickering hallway light illuminating his dark intentions. "Well, well, what a lovely reunion," he taunted, stepping inside without invitation. "I hope I'm not interrupting anything important."

"Get out, Paul," Ethan growled, standing between him and Sophie. "You don't belong here."

"Oh, but I think I do," Paul replied, pretending to be innocent. "And I think it's time for a little chat about boundaries."

"Talk? I'm not interested in your twisted games," Ethan spat, fists clenching at his sides, adrenaline coursing through him. "You need to leave."

Paul's grin faded, replaced by a dangerous glare. "You really think you can protect her?" he said, his tone darkening. "You're playing a dangerous game, Ethan, and you're about to lose."

Ethan's jaw tightened as he stepped closer, every instinct screaming to defend Sophie. "I'm not afraid of you."

"Good. Because you should be," Paul said with a smirk as he moved toward Ethan.

"Run!" Ethan shouted at Sophie, his instincts kicking in. "Get to your apartment! I'll deal with him."

Sophie hesitated, her eyes wide with fear. "Ethan, I won't leave you!"

"Go!" he insisted, desperation clawing at his chest. "I can't let you get hurt."

With a hesitant nod, she ran down the hall, her footsteps echoing against the walls, leaving Ethan and Paul face to face.

"Now, let's settle this," Paul sneered, charging at Ethan.

Ethan was ready. He sidestepped, delivering a powerful punch to Paul's jaw, feeling a rush of satisfaction with the hit. Paul stumbled back, surprised by Ethan's strength.

"You think you can take me on?" Paul taunted, wiping blood from his mouth as he regained his footing. "You'll regret this!"

Ethan charged forward again, adrenaline pumping through his veins, but Paul was quick. He dodged Ethan's attack and retaliated with a swift kick that sent Ethan crashing into the wall. Pain exploded in Ethan's side, but he gritted his teeth and pressed on.

The two men exchanged blows, fists flying in a chaotic dance of violence. Ethan fought fiercely, driven by the need to protect Sophie, to rid her of this nightmare. He felt powerful, in control, but the tide began to turn when Paul landed a well-aimed blow to Ethan's head with a nearby chair leg.

Dizziness hit Ethan, and the world around him started to fade. He staggered, struggling to maintain his balance, but darkness closed in as he collapsed to the floor.

Ethan awoke to a disorienting silence, the remnants of the fight fading from memory. Groggy and confused, he pushed himself up, the pounding in his head intensifying with each movement. "Sophie?" he croaked. The room was empty, the air thick with an unsettling stillness.

His bleary eyes scanned the dim space, his heart racing as faint signs of chaos came into focus, a chair tipped on its side, shards of glass scattered across the floor like jagged fragments of light. The weight of the silence pressed against him, thick and suffocating. He staggered to his feet, steadying himself against the wall, and called out again, louder this time. "Sophie, where are you?" His words hung in the air, unanswered, swallowed by the oppressive quiet."

He rushed down the hall to her apartment, knocking on doors and calling her name. Each unanswered knock shot a wave of anxiety through him. When he finally reached her door, he knocked urgently and shouted her name. "Sophie! It's me!"

Silence answered him, and dread filled his chest as he turned the doorknob and found it unlocked. Pushing the door open, he stepped inside and was met with an unsettling quiet in the room.

"Sophie?" he called again, his voice thick with urgency.

But the room was empty. The bed was neatly made, and the air felt heavy. Panic surged through Ethan as he scanned the room, desperately looking for any sign of her.

His heart sank when he spotted a suitcase near the closet, half-packed, with clothes tossed across the bed. A cold fear settled in his stomach as he stepped closer, the truth sinking in.

He turned to leave, his mind racing. "Sophie!" he shouted, desperation clawing at his throat. "Where are you?"

Just then, Sophie's flatmate, Jenna, appeared in the doorway, her face pale.

"Where's Sophie?" he asked, his voice thick with urgency. "Is she here?"

Jenna shook her head, a look of sorrow washing over her face. "She... she left. She packed up her things and went somewhere."

"What do you mean she left?" Ethan's heart sank as he struggled to comprehend her words. "Where did she go?"

"I don't know," Jenna replied, shaking her head. "She didn't tell me anything. Just that it was for the best."

Ethan felt the ground shift beneath him. "She can't just leave! Not like this!" He fought to suppress the rising panic, his mind racing. "Did she leave a note? Anything?"

Jenna hesitated, biting her lip as she handed him a folded piece of paper. "She wrote this for you," she said softly. "I tried to convince her to stay, but she was... resolute. She said it was the only way to keep you safe."

With trembling hands, Ethan unfolded the note, his heart pounding in his chest as he read Sophie's words:

"Ethan,

I love you more than I can express, but I need to do this. Paul won't stop until he gets what he wants, and I can't bear the thought of him coming after you again. I've packed everything and left. Please understand this is for your safety. You deserve a life free from this darkness. I hope one day you can forgive me.

Love always,

Sophie."

The words blurred as tears filled his eyes, the realization crashing down like a tidal wave. She was gone.

Each word felt like a knife twisting in his heart, the finality of her decision crashing down around him. Tears pricked at the corners of his eyes as he struggled to catch his breath. She really did leave.

"Ethan, I'm so sorry," Jenna said, her voice breaking as she placed a hand on his shoulder. "She was scared, and I think she felt like this was the only way."

"What do you mean she was scared?" Ethan's frustration bubbled to the surface. "Scared of what?"

"Paul," Jenna replied, her voice lowering. "She was terrified of him, Ethan. She thought leaving was the only way to keep you both safe."

Ethan felt a surge of anger rise within him, a fire igniting in his chest. "So she thinks running away will solve this? That it'll make Paul disappear?"

Jenna shook her head, her eyes filled with sympathy. "I don't think she knows what else to do. She felt trapped, and leaving seemed like her only option."

"Option?" he echoed, pacing the room. "She's leaving behind everything. I can't let her go like this! I need to find her."

"Ethan, wait," Jenna said, stepping in front of him. "You need to think this through. Paul is dangerous. You could put yourself at risk."

His fists tightened. "I can't just sit here! I have to find her!"

"Then what?" she asked, her voice rising. "You can't face Paul alone. He won't let you just walk away."

"I'll figure it out," he said firmly, determination flaring. "She needs me. I can't leave her alone."

"Ethan, please," Jenna pleaded, her voice thick with emotion. "If you go after her, it could make things worse. Paul is unpredictable."

"I don't care!" he shot back, his voice echoing in the silence. "I'd rather face him head-on than sit here and do nothing while she's out there alone."

"Just be careful," Jenna warned, the worry etched into her features. "Promise me you'll watch your back."

"I will," he said, determination igniting within him. "But I won't give up on Sophie. Not now. Not ever."

With that, he sprinted out of her apartment, adrenaline pumping through his veins as he raced back down the stairs and into the rain-soaked streets. Each drop felt like a reminder of his loss, each gust of wind a whisper of Sophie's absence.

As he moved through the darkened streets, thoughts raced through his mind. Where would she go?

He passed familiar landmarks—the coffee shop where they had shared countless laughs, the small diner where they'd spent late nights talking about their dreams. But now, everything felt empty, as if her leaving had left a shadow over everything.

She must be at the bus station.

Ethan hurried through the rain, each drop drenching him, matching the storm of emotions inside. His heart ached as he pushed forward, feeling the world closing in.

When he finally reached the bus station, he scanned the area, his heart pounding as he searched for any sign of her. The bright lights flickered above, but the waiting area was full of unfamiliar faces—no sign of her.

"Sophie!" he called, his voice echoing against the walls, desperation lacing his tone. "Sophie, where are you?"

He approached the ticket counter, breathless. "Has a girl with dark hair passed through here? She's about my height"

The attendant looked up, sympathy etched on her face. "I'm sorry, sir. I can't give out that information. But we have several buses leaving soon."

"Please," Ethan pleaded, leaning against the counter. "It's urgent. I need to find her."

The attendant looked around and spoke quietly. "I saw someone matching that description earlier. She seemed upset—like she was running away from something."

Ethan felt his heart drop. "Which bus did she take?"

"I'm not sure. She bought a ticket to Eastbrook, but I can't tell you exactly which one," the attendant said softly. "I'm really sorry."

"Thank you," Ethan said, the weight of his heartache settling in. He dashed outside into the storm once more, the rain pouring down, mixing with the tears that threatened to spill.

Eastbrook.

He had to hurry. He needed to catch her before it was too late.

The bus drove off just as Ethan arrived, and panic shot through him. He rushed to the ticket counter, breathless. "Is there another bus to Eastbrook soon?"

The attendant shook her head. "Not for another hour. You'll have to wait."

"No time to wait!" Ethan yelled, turning to sprint toward the parking lot. He would drive himself if he had to. He refused to let her go.

He fumbled for his keys, barely able to keep his hands steady as he started his car. The engine roared to life, and he sped off into the night, the rain pounding against the windshield. Thoughts raced through his mind as he navigated the familiar streets, each turn leading him further from Riverside and closer to finding Sophie.

With every mile he drove, the urgency in his heart intensified. What if she was already gone? What if she was with Paul?

He pushed the thoughts away, focusing instead on the road ahead. He had to find her.

As he drove, memories filled his mind—the laughter, the dreams they talked about, and the moments that brought them close. How had everything fallen apart so fast?

When he finally reached Eastbrook, he parked in front of the bus station and sprinted inside, scanning the area for any sign of Sophie. "Sophie!" he shouted, desperation echoing off the walls. "Where are you?"

But the station was just as empty as before. He felt the weight of despair pressing down on him, a suffocating blanket of hopelessness.

"Please!" he cried out, turning to the attendant at the counter. "Has anyone seen a girl with dark hair? She was just here. She couldn't have left!"

The attendant frowned, shaking her head. "I'm sorry. I haven't seen anyone like that. Are you sure she came this way?"

"Of course!" he snapped. "She wouldn't just disappear!"

"Sir, I need you to calm down," she said, her tone steady. "There's no need for panic."

Ethan took a deep breath, trying to hold his emotions. "I'm sorry. It's just... she means everything to me. I can't lose her."

The attendant softened, her expression changing to one of sympathy. "Maybe she's just at a nearby café. Sometimes people go to grab a drink or something before they leave."

Ethan nodded, holding onto her words like they were a lifeline. "Thank you."

He rushed out of the station and down the street, scanning the storefronts until he spotted a small café. He pushed the door open, a bell jingling overhead, and rushed inside.

The café was bustling, filled with the warm aroma of coffee and the chatter of patrons. His heart raced as he searched the room, but his hopes sank when he didn't see Sophie anywhere.

"Excuse me," he called to a waitress, desperation creeping into his voice. "Have you seen a girl with dark hair? She was just here."

The waitress paused, considering him. "Yeah, I saw someone who looked like that. She came in a while ago, but she left with a backpack."

"Which way did she go?" he asked, panic creeping into his voice.

"She went out the back door, toward the park," the waitress replied, pointing to a door at the rear of the café. "But she looked upset, like she was in a hurry."

"Thank you!" Ethan shouted, rushing out of the café and heading toward the park. The rain had eased to a drizzle, but the air was thick with tension as he sprinted down the path, desperation fueling his every step.

When he reached the park, he scanned the area, searching for any sign of her. "Sophie!" he called, his voice echoing through the trees. "Where are you?"

The park was dimly lit, shadows dancing along the path. Ethan's heart raced as he walked deeper into the park, the wind rustling the leaves overhead, whispering secrets he desperately wanted to uncover.

Suddenly, he spotted a girl in the distance—a silhouette standing alone beneath a large oak tree. His heart raced as he moved closer, the shape growing clearer with each step.

"Sophie?" he called out, hope flaring in his chest.

As he got closer, the girl turned, and his heart sank. It wasn't Sophie; it was another girl with long, dark hair, her expression a mix of surprise and concern. "Who are you?" she asked, taken aback by his sudden approach.

Ethan's heart dropped, disappointment washing over him like a cold wave. "Sorry," he murmured, breathless. "I thought you were someone else."

"Are you okay?" she asked, eyeing him with worry as the rain continued to pour down.

"I'm fine," he replied, forcing the words out. But the truth was far from it, he felt anything but fine. Panic clawed at his insides. "I'm just looking for someone."

The girl frowned, glancing around as if hoping to see Sophie appear. "You look upset. Is she missing?"

"Yes," Ethan admitted. "Her name is Sophie. I think she's here in Eastbrook, but I don't know where she's staying."

The girl shook her head, sympathy crossing her features. "I'm sorry. I haven't seen her. But you might want to check another café down the road. People often go there to escape the rain."

"Thanks," he said, but the words felt hollow. He turned away, feeling the weight of disappointment settling in his chest. Where could she be?

With determination, he pressed on down the path, his desperation driving each step. The rain poured down, soaking him to the bone, but he barely noticed. All that mattered was finding Sophie and bringing her back.

When he finally reached the café, he rushed through the door, feeling a wave of warmth and the rich scent of coffee wash over him. Yet, everything felt different without Sophie there. He quickly looked around the room, but she was nowhere to be found.

"Excuse me," he called to the barista, his heart racing. "Have you seen a girl with dark hair? She was just here."

The barista looked up, worry on her face. "I'm sorry, but I haven't seen anyone like that."

Ethan felt his heart sink further, fear creeping in. "Are you sure?"

She shook her head gently. "But I can keep an eye out. Do you want to leave your number?"

"No," he said. "I need to find her now."

With that, he rushed out of the café. Where could she have gone?

Ethan stopped at the edge of the park, scanning the area, hoping to see her face, but there was nothing. "Sophie!" he shouted, desperation echoing in the stillness.

But as the rain fell around him, he felt an overwhelming sense of loss. She was gone, and with her, a part of him felt forever lost.

He pushed himself up and walked to his car parked nearby. He opened the door and climbed inside, slamming it shut against the storm. The rain drummed loudly on the roof, matching the chaos in his mind.

He sat in the driver's seat, gripping the steering wheel tightly. The interior was warm, but it felt heavy with despair. He glanced out the window, watching the rain streak down the glass, making the world outside look blurry. Where could she possibly be?

Ethan needed to keep searching. He had to believe that he could find her before it was too late.

He took a deep breath and turned the ignition, the engine roaring to life. This wasn't over.

Chapter Six

A DAYDREAM OF LIGHT

Ethan was driving along the roads to Eastbrook, searching for Sophie. Each day felt bittersweet—a journey to the heart of the girl who had captured his soul: Sophie. Familiar roads sparked memories of their laughter and shared moments. The air was thick with reminders of her, making it hard to forget what he had to lose.

Today, he felt restless and took a different route through quaint neighbourhoods, searching for any sign of Sophie, each one seeming to whisper secrets of romance and adventure.

Charming houses lined the streets, each one full of potential. Could this be her home? Each door held the hope of what could be—a place where he could knock and find Sophie waiting for him, her smile bright enough to light up even the gloomiest day.

He slowed in front of a brick house draped in ivy, the warm glow of the setting sun bathing everything in light. Could this be the one? Maybe Sophie was inside, curled up by the window, lost in a book or dreaming of far-off places, her imagination as bright as the flowers in the garden.

Excitement filled his chest, urging him to pull over. He parked the car, his heart racing with every thought. What if she really was inside? He stepped out into the cool evening air, feeling it brush against his skin like a gentle touch, and walked toward the house, each step filled with a mix of hope and worry.

Standing there, he imagined the moment she might appear. Would she peek out, eyes sparkling with that familiar mischief that made his heart skip? What would he say? Would he stammer, or would he confidently declare, "Hey, Sophie, it's me. I've been wandering these streets just to find you"?

Each step taking him deeper into the neighbourhood. The air was filled with the sounds of rustling leaves. He wandered without a plan, looking into windows and imagining her life behind each one. Was she laughing with friends? Was she curled up with a book, lost in her thoughts?

Turning a corner, he found a beautiful house with an elegant and welcoming design. The warm light spilling from the windows drew him closer, stirring a sudden longing inside him. What if she was inside, just a few steps away?

His heart raced as he felt like fate was guiding him. He took a deep breath, excitement filling the air, and crossed the street, the soft crunch of gravel under his shoes breaking the evening silence.

His mind buzzed with possibilities, imagining different ways he might find her. Would she greet him with surprise, her laughter filling the night air? Would she rush into his arms, her warmth easing the pain of being apart? As he approached the front door, he pictured it in his mind. "I've searched everywhere, Sophie, just to be here with you." The thought made him smile, a mix of hope and excitement bubbling in his chest.

Then, just as the world felt alive with potential, a flicker of movement caught his eye— a girl, ethereal like an angel. Could it be? Ethan's heart raced, and he leaned forward, anticipation coursing through him like electricity.

As the figure stepped out of the house, the warm light from the windows surrounded her, highlighting her delicate features and stunning beauty. With each step she took, it felt like time slowed down, and everything else around him disappeared. She moved down the stairs like she was floating, each step feeling like a gentle promise of something amazing. Ethan realized with a rush of emotion that it was Sophie, and the sight of her took his breath away.

Ethan stood there, completely captivated, caught between disbelief and the powerful truth of her presence. She looked like a dream come to life, too perfect to be real. Her smile was like sunlight breaking through dark clouds, lighting up the shadows in his heart and warming the cool evening air around him.

"Hey there," Sophie called, her voice playful and melodic, a soothing balm against the aching loneliness he often felt. "You look like you've just seen a star fall."

"Only if you're the star," Ethan replied, his heart fluttering in response to her playful banter. She laughed softly, the sound dancing in the air, wrapping him in a warm cocoon of happiness.

As she approached, their eyes locked, and everything else faded away—the world around them became a blur. He was lost in the depth of her gaze, feeling as though he could drown in the warmth of her smile. Her beauty was a gentle spell, casting aside all worries and doubts.

"I was starting to think you'd never show up," she teased, her eyes sparkling. Her playful tone made Ethan's heart race.

"Well, I guess I just needed the right motivation," he said, stepping closer, his confidence growing with her smile. "And here you are, making my day brighter."

Sophie beamed, the sunlight reflecting off her hair, making her look like a goddess. "Well, I hope to be the highlight of your day, Ethan

Hart. But I'm curious—what else do you have planned for our time together?"

As they stood close, the space between them crackled with unspoken words, electricity buzzing in the air. He could hardly think straight; the mere sight of her made the world fade into a background hum.

"I was hoping we could explore a little," he said, trying to keep his voice steady. "Maybe find a place where the stars are brighter, where we can hear the night sing."

Her eyes sparkled with mischief. "A romantic adventure, you say? Count me in! Just lead the way, and I'll follow."

With that, they decided to take a drive around the city. The lights sparkled like stars spread across a wide sky. As they drove through the calm streets, the cool breeze flowed around them, wrapping them in a warm embrace. Every moment they shared felt like a special gift, one he hoped would last forever.

"You're the best company I've ever had," Ethan said, glancing at her with admiration, as if she were the answer to every question he'd ever asked.

Sophie leaned in closer, her smile warm and inviting. "And you're not so bad yourself," she winked, her playful attitude making his heart skip a beat. The closeness sent a thrill through him, igniting a longing that had taken root deep in his heart.

They turned onto a scenic route lined with trees, their branches swaying gently in the breeze as if they were welcoming the couple into their embrace. The leaves rustled softly, creating a soothing sound that felt like nature's applause. The streetlights flickered above, casting a warm glow on their faces as if the universe were blessing their moment together.

"You know," Sophie began, her voice softening, "there's something magical about nights like this. Everything feels more alive, more vibrant. It's like the world is holding its breath, waiting for something wonderful to happen."

Ethan nodded, the weight of her words sinking into his heart. "Every moment with you feels like a gift. It's like I've been wandering in a desert, and suddenly, there's an oasis. You make everything better."

Sophie smiled, her cheeks flushed with warmth. "That's sweet of you to say. I feel the same way. I've never felt so... free." She looked out at the passing scenery, the city lights twinkling like stars fallen to earth.

As they continued driving, they came across a small park nestled between the houses. The park was bathed in a silvery glow from the moonlight, the grass shimmering like jewels. "Let's stop here," Sophie suggested, her eyes lighting up with excitement. "I want to show you something."

Ethan parked the car, and they stepped into the cool night air. The sweet fragrance of blooming flowers surrounded them, intoxicating and fresh. As they walked hand in hand through the park, a deep sense of peace washed over Ethan.

Sophie led him to a clearing where the trees parted to reveal a stunning view of the night sky. Stars twinkled above, sparkling like diamonds scattered across the vast darkness. She looked up, her face filled with pure wonder. "Isn't it beautiful?"

"It's stunning," Ethan replied, captivated not just by the sky but by her joy. "But you make it even more breathtaking."

Sophie turned to him, her eyes sparkling with delight. "You really know how to flatter a girl, don't you?"

"It's not flattery if it's true," he said, stepping closer, the warmth radiating from her making him feel alive. "You bring light into the darkest corners of my life."

"Is that so?" she teased, a playful smile dancing on her lips. "Then tell me, what would you do without me?"

Ethan chuckled at the thought of a world without her. "Honestly? I'd probably be a lost soul, drifting in darkness. But you... you shine so brightly that it's impossible not to be drawn to you."

As they drove, the connection between them felt alive, charged with a spark that made the air inside the car hum with excitement. He could feel her warmth beside him, the magnetic pull drawing him closer. "I'm so glad we met," Sophie said softly, her eyes searching his. "You make me feel alive. It's like I've been waiting for you without even knowing it."

"You're not alone in that," Ethan replied. "Meeting you has changed everything for me. You've shown me how beautiful life can be."

They shared dreams, fears, and secrets that felt like precious gems, each laugh echoing through the car like a melody that wrapped around them in a warm embrace. But then, as if the universe had shifted, Ethan heard the distant wail of an ambulance siren cutting through the intimacy of their moment.

"Did you hear that?" he asked, suddenly alert, his heart pounding in his chest. The sound floated through the air, mingling with the warmth of their conversation, turning their beautiful moment into a tangled web of uncertainty.

Sophie shook her head, her smile unwavering. "I don't hear anything. Just enjoy this moment with me," she urged, her voice soothing like a warm hug, but a flutter of unease still settled in the pit of his stomach.

As Ethan turned to look back at her, the light surrounding Sophie flickered like a candle in a storm. Then, in an instant, she disappeared, leaving the car dark and silent. The warmth that had filled the space vanished, leaving him feeling cold and empty inside. Panic surged through him as he faced forward again, a wave of dread washing over him, making it hard to breathe.

The world around him became a blur, and then, suddenly, he was hit by a blinding light and an overwhelming force.

Ethan's mind screamed as he felt the impact, the world collapsing into chaos around him. The reality of the accident crashed into him like a wave, pulling him under. He was hit by a car, he realized in the last fleeting moments of consciousness before everything went dark.

As he lay on the pavement, agony coursing through his body, his vision blurred. In that moment, he caught a glimpse of movement. There was Sophie, running toward him, her face filled with fear and determination. "Ethan!" Her voice rang out like a lifeline amidst the chaos.

But just as hope surged within him, a tall, old man stepped in front of her, blocking her path. "No, stay back!" he commanded, gripping her arm tightly.

Sophie tried to cross the road to reach Ethan, desperation written all over her face. "Let me go! I have to help him!" she pleaded, her voice trembling with urgency. But the old man held firm, pulling her away as if the universe were trying to keep them apart.

Ethan's heart sank as he watched Sophie fight against the man's grasp. He strained to call out to her, but his words faded into a breathless whisper, lost in the darkness that surrounded him.

In those last moments, he felt caught between reality and illusion. Sophie's figure blurred before him, her worried expression etched into his mind. Then, just as quickly as she appeared, she vanished, swallowed by the shadows.

As his consciousness slipped away, he held onto the image of her, but the feeling of her presence faded, like sand slipping through his fingers. Then, everything went dark.

When Ethan opened his eyes, the scent of antiseptic filled the air, and the soft, steady beeps of machines surrounded him. He lay in a hospital bed, the walls around him unfamiliar and cold. His mind felt hazy, the details of the evening blurry and out of reach. Sophie... The memories came back slowly, like pieces of a puzzle scattered in the wind.

"Where... am I?", his voice rough and barely audible. The dim light in the room flickered, casting shifting shadows across the walls. As he turned his head, struggling to make sense of it all, a familiar face appeared beside him.

"Hey, buddy," a voice called out, filled with relief and warmth.

Ethan squinted, his heart racing as he recognized the figure sitting beside him. It was Jake, an old friend from high school, someone he hadn't seen in years. They had lost touch after graduation, life pulling them in different directions, but Ethan remembered their countless adventures.

"Jake? What happened?" Ethan struggled to sit up, a wave of dizziness washing over him.

"You were in an accident," Jake explained, his voice steady but filled with concern. "I was just passing by when I saw you lying on the ground. I didn't know it was you at first. I thought I'd lost you."

Ethan's heart sank at the thought of what could have happened. "How did it happen? I was just... with Sophie."

Jake's expression turned worried. "You were lying in the street when I found you. I don't know everything, but it looked serious. I called an ambulance right away. You've been unconscious for a couple of days."

"Days?" Ethan repeated, a sinking feeling growing in his stomach. He had been dreaming about Sophie, about their time together, and now… now he was here, far away from her.

"Yeah, they were worried about your head injury," Jake continued, leaning closer, his expression serious. "But you're going to be okay, man. You just need to take it easy."

Ethan's mind raced with worry. Sophie—what had happened to her? Did she know? Would she come to see him? The thought of her, the light of his life, filled him with a desperate need to reach her.

"Is Sophie, okay?" he asked, urgency creeping into his voice. "She's the girl I was with. I need to know she's safe."

Jake hesitated, his gaze dropping as if he were trying to find the right words. "No, Ethan, I didn't see anyone else in the car. It was just you who was injured."

A chill settled in Ethan's stomach, and he felt panic rising. Was he just imagining Sophie? The thought hit him hard, leaving him unsure if his heart was deceiving him.

Jake, sensing the tension, tried to lighten the mood. "Man, you love someone so much that you're daydreaming about her," he joked gently. "You really need to focus on getting better before you start creating a whole new story in your head."

Ethan managed a weak smile, grateful for Jake's attempt at humour. Yet, the worry lingered. "I just want to know she's okay."

Ethan struggled against the hospital sheets, a wave of frustration coursing through him. "I can't just sit here. I need to find her! She was right there with me. We were... we were together!"

"Look," Jake said, trying to keep his voice steady, "I get it. But you need to be realistic. Sometimes things don't work out the way we hope. Love... it can be complicated."

Ethan's heart ached at the thought, the memory of Sophie's laughter ringing in his ears. "What do you mean? Love is worth fighting for, isn't it? You can't just throw it away."

Jake looked at him, his expression serious. "I know it feels that way, but sometimes people get hurt. And sometimes it's better to let go before you lose everything. You can't keep clinging to something that might not be there anymore."

As the reality of his situation settled in, Ethan recalled why he had come to Eastbrook—he had been searching for Sophie. He had been driving through the neighbourhood, filled with hope and memories, before everything went dark and he met with the accident. Was it possible that meeting Sophie and driving with her through these streets had all been a figment of his imagination?

Jake, noticing the pain etched on Ethan's face, leaned forward slightly. "Hey, it's okay to feel confused. You've been through a lot. Just remember, if it felt real to you, then it matters. Focus on getting better, and we'll figure this out together."

The words hung heavily between them, filled with unspoken feelings. Ethan felt Jake's concern and the bond of their friendship. Yet beneath that weight was a flicker of hope that wouldn't go out. He had to believe that love could overcome anything and that Sophie was worth fighting for.

"Even if things don't work out, I'll always cherish our moments together," Ethan said firmly. "You can't just forget someone like that. You hold onto those memories and fight for them."

Jake nodded, respect shining in his eyes. "I get it. Just promise me you'll take it one step at a time and focus on getting better."

Ethan let out a breath he didn't realize he was holding. "Yeah, I promise."

Days passed in the hospital, the steady beeping of machines providing a backdrop to his thoughts. During those moments of solitude, he often found himself staring at the ceiling. He thought about their time together—the love they shared, the long walks, the stolen moments. Those moments felt like treasures, each one a precious memory he held onto as he faced the challenges of his recovery.

The memories from Riverside were real. But after Paul's threats forced Sophie to disappear, Ethan's need for her had blurred the lines between reality and longing. In Eastbrook, his mind had filled in the emptiness with her presence, making him believe she was still with him, sitting by his side. But she wasn't.

His heart ached as the realization hit him. The conversations, the laughter, the comfort she brought—those were just pieces of a daydream, created by his longing to see her again. The accident had been real, but Sophie's presence in Eastbrook had only been an illusion.

Sophie hadn't been with him in Eastbrook. Not in the way he'd imagined.

But as he lay there now in the hospital bed, a different memory crossed his mind—a memory from just after the accident.

After the car hit him, while he lay on the cold ground, dazed and barely conscious, he saw her. Sophie was on the other side of the road, her eyes wide with fear and her hands reaching out to him as if she wanted to cross. But an old man, tall and shadowed in the fading light, had held her back, refusing to let her cross.

Was it real?

He squeezed his eyes shut, frustration and confusion swirling inside him. He wanted to believe she had been there, that Sophie had seen him and wanted to come to him. But the haze of the accident, the mix of pain and disorientation—it made everything feel like fragments of a broken memory, impossible to piece together.

As he lay in the sterile hospital bed, the machines beeping softly around him, he couldn't be sure. Was she truly there, or was this yet another cruel daydream crafted by his aching mind? Another figment of his imagination, just like her presence in the car?

Chapter Seven

ECHOES OF THE PAST

Sophie stood at the window of her small apartment in Eastbrook, the setting sun casting a warm glow across the city. The vibrant colours painted the sky in shades of orange and pink, but the beauty outside felt empty to her. She had come here to escape the darkness of her past, yet the weight of anxiety pressed heavily on her chest.

Her thoughts drifted back to that day—the day of the accident that had shattered everything.

<u>Flashback: The Day of the Accident</u>

The memory of that day was etched into her mind. It had been a bright afternoon in Eastbrook, the sun shining down as Sophie walked through the bustling streets, anticipation bubbling within her.

But as she got closer to the intersection, everything changed. She saw Ethan's car parked awkwardly at the curb, and a feeling of unease settled in her stomach.

Just as she had decided to cross, her dad stepped in front of her, blocking her path with an unyielding stance. "Not yet, dear," he had said, his voice calm but firm. "Wait for the light."

"Please, let me go!" she cried, desperation filling her words as she fought against him. "I need to get to him!"

But her dad's grip held her back, and panic surged within her as the seconds ticked away. She watched the light change, her heart pounding in her chest.

There he lay, crumpled on the asphalt, his body limp and vulnerable. Seeing him like that sent shockwaves through Sophie. Sirens wailed in the distance, but all she heard was the rush of blood in her ears.

"Ethan!" she cried, "Please, don't leave me!"

But he remained silent, confusion and pain etched on his face. Sophie felt helpless, drowning in despair. Around her, chaos erupted as paramedics arrived and began to assess the scene, but all she could focus on was Ethan, lying there in pain.

The Guilt

Now, standing in Eastbrook, the guilt washed over her like a tidal wave. If only she had crossed the road faster. If only she had been strong enough to push past her dad. Each thought twisted in her gut, a reminder of her powerlessness.

Days turned into weeks, and while Ethan was healing, Sophie felt trapped in a whirlwind of worry and regret. The memories replayed in her mind like a broken record, each note a painful reminder of what had happened. She could still see his face, his laughter replaced by confusion and pain, the life drained from him in an instant.

Would Paul come for Ethan? Would he find a way to destroy everything she had fought for? These questions clawed at her, tightening their grip on her heart. The shadows of her past loomed large, threatening to engulf her once more.

Sophie took a deep breath, trying to steady herself against the rising tide of emotions. She pressed her palms against the cool glass of the window, feeling the chill seep into her bones. She couldn't let fear consume her; she had to confront the truth.

Determined not to let her past dictate her future, Sophie stepped outside, the cool evening air wrapping around her like a shroud. Each step toward the park felt heavy with the weight of her memories, but she refused to let them control her. She had to face whatever awaited her.

As she walked through the park, the cherry blossoms swayed gently in the breeze, their delicate petals fluttering like fragile hopes. The distant laughter of children playing filled the air, a stark contrast to the chaos swirling within her.

Sophie paused under a cherry blossom tree, its branches swaying gracefully above her. She closed her eyes, allowing herself a moment to breathe. The warmth of the sun on her skin felt almost comforting, but the chill of reality quickly returned.

Ethan had come all this way to find her, only to end up in danger. The thought of him lying in pain because of her past decisions twisted her heart with guilt. She had to be strong for him; she couldn't let her fears dictate their future.

With determination, Sophie opened her eyes and continued walking, her mind racing with thoughts of how to confront her fears. She wouldn't let Paul ruin her chance at happiness. For Ethan, she would face whatever darkness lay ahead.

Chapter Eight

THE BLOOM OF FOREVER

Days passed in the hospital as Ethan gradually regained his strength. The room was bright with cold, sterile light, and the steady beeping of machines filled the air. Each time he opened his eyes, he saw the pale ceiling above him, a sight that had become all too familiar. Though his mind sometimes felt foggy from the medication, clarity began to return. His chest still ached—not just from his injuries, but from a deep, lingering longing for Sophie.

And then, finally, the day came when he was discharged. Jake was there to pick him up, a reassuring presence amidst the haze of medical staff and equipment. Ethan stepped out of the hospital, the sunlight hitting his face like a warm embrace. It felt good to be free, but his heart raced with uncertainty.

"Ready to face the world again?" Jake asked, his voice light, trying to lift the mood.

Ethan nodded, though anxiety bubbled beneath the surface. "Yeah, but I need to find Sophie. I have to know how she's doing."

"Let's take it one step at a time," Jake replied, a knowing look in his eyes.

They drove to Jake's home in Eastbrook, where Ethan could recover further in a familiar setting. Days passed as he rested, allowing his body to heal.

One sunny afternoon, feeling a bit stronger, Ethan found himself wandering through the park in Eastbrook. The cherry blossoms were in full bloom, their delicate petals drifting down like snowflakes, covering the path in soft pink. The air was thick with the scent of flowers, and the laughter of children echoed in the distance, a joyful noise that felt distant, almost unreal to him.

And then, he saw her.

Sophie.

She was standing beneath the canopy of a cherry blossom tree, her dark hair catching the golden light of the setting sun. For a moment, Ethan thought his mind was playing tricks on him. He had dreamed of this so many times—of seeing her again, of running into her like it was fate. But as he blinked and stared, the reality of her presence began to sink in.

His heart quickened, his feet moving on their own as he crossed the path, his eyes never leaving her. "Sophie…" he whispered, breathless.

She turned, her eyes widening in surprise as they locked onto his. For a heartbeat, they stood frozen, staring at each other across the space that had once been filled with so much distance, so much silence.

Then, she smiled—a smile that made Ethan's chest tighten in the best possible way. "Ethan?" she said softly, as if she couldn't quite believe he was standing there.

A soft, disbelieving laugh escaped him as he took a step closer. "You're alive," he said, the relief and joy flooding his voice.

Her eyes filled with warmth and a touch of amusement. "You're alive too," she replied, her voice trembling with emotion. She took a step toward him, the distance between them shrinking. "I thought I'd lost you."

"I've been dreaming about you," Ethan confessed, his voice low, filled with the weight of the months they had spent apart. "You know, I almost had a heart attack when I saw you running toward me that night."

Sophie's soft laughter filled the air like a melody, wrapping around him, making the world feel lighter. "I was so confused! When my dad pulled me back, I thought I was losing my mind. I just wanted to reach you."

His hands found hers, his touch gentle but firm, as if anchoring her to him, making sure she was real. "I thought I'd never see you again," he whispered, his voice cracking with vulnerability. "But here you are… like a dream I never want to wake from."

Her smile widened, and a soft blush coloured her cheeks as the meaning of his words settled in. In that moment, she understood that falling for him meant finding herself in all of his creations, woven into every word, every story, forever a part of his world.

As the sun dipped below the horizon, casting a warm glow around them, the world fell away, leaving just the two of them in their own little bubble of magic. The air was thick with the scent of cherry blossoms, and the laughter of children faded into the background, replaced by the soft rhythm of their heartbeats.

Ethan took a step closer, the warmth of her presence enveloping him. "You know," he began, his voice soft but teasing, "I think this moment deserves something special."

Sophie looked up at him, her eyes reflecting the soft colours of the sunset. "What do you mean?"

Ethan reached out, gently tucking a loose strand of hair behind her ear, his fingers brushing against her skin. "Just this," he whispered. "Being here with you, sharing this moment."

Her breath caught in her throat, and Ethan saw the surprise in her eyes as she leaned into his touch. "It feels magical," she said softly, her voice filled with awe.

"Exactly," Ethan said, his heart racing. "It's like we're the only two people in the world right now."

They stood in silence, the air thick with unspoken words, their hearts beating in sync. Ethan slowly took her hand, intertwining their fingers, feeling the warmth of her skin against his.

"Whatever happens next," he murmured, his voice filled with emotion, "I want you to know that this moment means everything to me."

Sophie's smile widened, and she squeezed his hand gently. "Me too," she said, her voice barely above a whisper. "It feels like the start of something beautiful."

Ethan gazed into her eyes, seeing the depth of her emotions reflected there. "When I look at you, I see a future filled with possibilities. A future where we chase our dreams together, hand in hand."

Sophie's cheeks flushed a deeper shade of pink as she stepped closer. "I want that too. A future where we create our own path, no matter what obstacles come our way."

They stood there, lost in each other's eyes, the world around them fading into insignificance. In that moment, it felt like they were the only two people who mattered, connected by a bond that transcended time and space.

As they began to walk, hand in hand, down the path lined with cherry blossoms, Ethan felt a peace settle over him that he hadn't felt in months. For the first time in what felt like an eternity, everything was right in the world. He had Sophie by his side, the promise of a future filled with love and adventure stretched out before them. The past was behind them, and the only thing that mattered now was the present—their present, their love.

Sophie's cheeks flushed a deeper shade of pink as she stepped closer, her voice dropping to a whisper. "How much do you love me?"

Ethan's heart soared at her question, and he opened his mouth to respond, wanting to pour out all the feelings that swelled within him. "I love you like—"

But just as they turned onto a quieter path, the warm glow of the setting sun casting long shadows around them, the air was shattered by a sharp, piercing sound.

It was a gunshot.

Ethan barely had time to register the noise before he felt the impact—a searing pain exploding in his chest. His body jolted violently, and the world around him seemed to tilt on its axis. The warm, peaceful park, the soft colours of the sunset, Sophie's hand in his—all of it blurred into a chaotic whirl of confusion and pain.

His legs buckled beneath him, and before he knew it, he was on the ground, the cold concrete hard beneath him. He gasped for breath, the pain spreading through his body like fire, each beat of his heart sending waves of agony crashing over him.

"Ethan!" Sophie's voice was filled with terror as she dropped to her knees beside him, her hands pressed desperately against his chest, trying to stop the blood that was quickly soaking through his shirt. "No, no, no! Please, Ethan, stay with me!"

Through the haze of pain, Ethan's eyes flickered open, his vision blurring at the edges. And standing just beyond the trees, cloaked in the growing darkness, was Paul.

The man who had haunted their lives, the man who had always lingered in the shadows, waiting for the perfect moment to strike. Paul stood there, his expression cold and mocking, the gun still in his hand.

"You really thought you could escape me?" Paul's voice was low and menacing, filled with a cruel satisfaction that sent a chill down Sophie's spine. He took a step closer, his eyes locked on Ethan's crumpled form, his smile widening. "I told you, Sophie. He's not yours to keep."

Sophie's breath hitched as she turned to Paul, her body trembling with fear and fury. "You monster," she spat, her voice shaking. "You've ruined everything!"

Paul's smile never wavered. "No, Sophie. I just reminded you of reality."

Without another word, Paul turned and disappeared into the darkness, leaving nothing but the echo of his cruel laughter behind.

Sophie's hands trembled as she pressed harder against Ethan's wound, her tears falling onto his chest, mixing with the blood. "Ethan, please," she sobbed, her voice breaking. "Please don't leave me. Stay with me. I need you."

Ethan could barely hear her. The world around him was fading, and the sounds of the park and Sophie's touch felt distant, like a dream slipping away. The pain was still there, but it was fading too, replaced by a cold feeling.

His eyes fluttered shut, and for a moment, everything was quiet.

But then, through the fog of his fading consciousness, he heard her. Sophie's voice, calling his name, begging him to stay. He wanted to— God, how he wanted to stay with her. But he could feel it, the pull of something greater, something beyond this moment.

"A… sleeping… eight," he whispered in response to Sophie's question, "How much do you love me?" His voice was so faint that he wasn't sure if she heard him.

Sophie's breath caught, confusion flashing across her tear-streaked face. "What? Ethan, no, please…"

But Ethan couldn't respond. His body felt heavy, his heart slowing with each passing second. The world was slipping away, and there was nothing he could do to stop it.

Chapter Nine

SHADOWS OF HOPE

The park, once vibrant with life and laughter, transformed into a desolate landscape, a stage for the chaos that had just unfolded. Sophie's heart raced as she pressed her hands against Ethan's wound, her fingers trembling in fear. Each drop of blood was a testament to her worst nightmare, and she couldn't bear the thought of losing him.

"Ethan, please!" she cried, her voice breaking as tears streamed down her face. "Stay with me! Help is on the way!" Panic surged within her, a tidal wave of fear threatening to consume her.

Ethan lay there, his breathing shallow and erratic, and she could see the flicker of consciousness slowly fading from his eyes. "No, no, no," she whispered, her heart shattering as the reality of the situation set in. "Don't you dare leave me. I need you. You promised me, Ethan. We have a future together."

As she knelt there, time stretched on endlessly. The distant sounds of sirens echoed in her ears, but they felt so far away, like a dream she couldn't quite grasp. She leaned down, her forehead resting against his, desperate to connect with him, to remind him that he wasn't alone.

"Ethan," she whispered, her voice barely audible. "Fight for me. Please. I can't do this without you. I love you." The confession hung in the air, raw and real.

Suddenly, Ethan's eyes fluttered open, and he blinked slowly, trying to focus on her face. "Sophie?" he whispered, his voice barely a breath.

"I'm here," she replied, her voice thick with emotion. "I'm right here. Just hold on a little longer."

His gaze locked onto hers, confusion and pain swirling in his eyes. "It hurts... so much..."

"I know, love," she murmured, brushing her fingers along his cheek, wishing she could take away the pain. "But you're going to be okay. Help is coming. Just keep looking at me."

Moments later, the distant wail of sirens grew louder, cutting through the thick fog of despair. Sophie's heart surged with relief as she heard the familiar sound. Paramedics burst onto the scene, their faces a mix of urgency and concern.

"Get an ambulance here, now!" one of the paramedics shouted as they rushed to Ethan's side. Sophie felt a surge of anxiety as they assessed his condition, their hands moving with practiced efficiency.

"Stay with us, Ethan!" one of the paramedics urged, applying pressure to his wound. "You're going to be okay. We're here to help."

Sophie stepped back, allowing the professionals to do their work, but her heart remained tethered to Ethan. "You hear that? You're going to be okay," she said, squeezing his hand tightly, unwilling to let go.

Ethan's eyes darted between her and the paramedics, confusion still clouding his features. "Sophie... I—"

"Shh, don't talk," she interrupted gently. "Just focus on me."

As the paramedics worked, the world around Sophie faded again, the sounds muffled. All she could focus on was Ethan, the warmth of his hand in hers, the way his eyes searched hers for reassurance.

"Promise me," he whispered, his voice strained. "Promise me you won't let him win."

Sophie's heart ached at the vulnerability in his words. "I promise, Ethan. I won't let Paul take you from me. We'll face him together."

With that promise hanging in the air, Ethan's eyes flickered shut, and Sophie felt her heart sink. "No, no, no! Ethan! Stay with me!"

She could see the paramedics rushing to help, but all her focus was on Ethan's body, which began to slump. The light in his eyes was fading. "Ethan, please! Don't you dare give up on me!"

Suddenly, one of the paramedics shouted, "We need to stabilize him! He's losing too much blood!"

Sophie's heart raced as she watched them connect him to a heart monitor. The beeping was steady, but each sound sent waves of fear coursing through her.

"Ethan!" she cried, tears streaming down her cheeks. "Please stay with me! You can't leave me. I love you!"

In that moment, as the sirens wailed and chaos surrounded them, Ethan's eyes fluttered open one last time. "Sophie… forever…" he whispered, the words escaping his lips like a final promise, a delicate thread binding their souls together even in this darkest hour.

And then, the world around her shattered.

As the sirens faded and the chaos settled, Sophie knelt on the ground, holding the spot where Ethan had fallen. The warmth of his hand disappeared, leaving a deep, unbearable cold in its place. Grief washed over her like a tidal wave, relentless and suffocating.

"No, Ethan! Please don't leave me!" she cried, her voice a desperate plea swallowed by the silence that followed. "I can't do this without you! You promised we'd face the darkness together!"

But he was gone. His final thought, as the darkness claimed him, was of Sophie—her laughter, her smile, the warmth of her hand in his. Their love was infinite. Forever.

The reality settled in around her like a heavy fog, wrapping around her heart and squeezing it until she could barely breathe. The tears flowed freely, a torrent of sorrow that felt never-ending.

In that moment of heartbreak, she felt the echoes of their love reverberate through the silence. A love that transcended time and space—a love that would forever be etched in her heart. "A Sleeping Eight," she whispered to the universe, a reminder that their love was infinite, eternal, and unbreakable. No matter the distance or the darkness that threatened to consume her, she would carry him with her, a part of her very soul.

As the first stars began to twinkle in the twilight sky, Sophie knelt where Ethan had once been. In her heart, she could still hear his laughter, feel his warmth, and see the promise of their shared dreams dancing in the stars above.

Though he had left this world, their love would forever illuminate the path ahead—a beacon of hope guiding her through the shadows. But the light felt dimmer now, and the world appeared less vibrant without him.

Days turned into weeks, and Sophie found herself lost in a haze of grief. The park was filled with memories—each corner a reminder of their laughter, their dreams, their love. Yet in the depths of her sorrow, a flicker of determination began to stir. She realized that to honour Ethan, she had to face her grief head-on.

With each passing day, she forced herself to step outside, to breathe the air that they had once shared. She spoke his name into the wind, whispered her love into the night sky, and learned to find solace in the beauty around her. Slowly, she began to reclaim her life, one small step at a time.

Sophie started volunteering at a local shelter, helping others who had experienced loss. In their pain, she found her own healing, connecting with people who understood the depths of sorrow. Through their stories, she felt Ethan's spirit guiding her, reminding her of the importance of love and connection.

In a moment of quiet reflection, Sophie returned to the cherry blossom tree where they had shared so many precious moments. The blossoms swayed gently in the breeze, their delicate petals dancing like memories in the wind. As she sat beneath the tree, she allowed herself to grieve fully, releasing the tears she had held back for so long.

"Ethan, I will carry you with me always," she promised, the breeze carrying her words into the ether. She walked forward, ready to face a new beginning, knowing that love never truly dies—it transforms, and in that transformation, it lives on.

Sophie stood beneath the cherry blossoms, letting the soft petals fall around her like gentle rain, each one a whisper of love carried by the wind. She took a deep breath, the sweet scent of the flowers filling her lungs, reminding her of the beauty that once filled her life.

"I will live for us both," she vowed, her voice steady despite the tremor of her heart. "Your love will be my compass, guiding me through the shadows and into the light."

As the sun dipped below the horizon, it painted the sky in radiant hues of orange and pink, a canvas of hope illuminating the twilight. Sophie felt a flicker of warmth begin to blossom within her heart, a flicker that pushed against the encroaching darkness. With every beat, it whispered promises of new beginnings and uncharted paths.

Though the road ahead was uncertain and fraught with challenges, she stood resolute, ready to embrace whatever came next. Armed with the profound knowledge that love is like "A Sleeping Eight"—

endless, infinite, and ever-present—Sophie understood that true connection transcends time and space.

With a final glance at the cherry blossoms swirling around her, she smiled softly, knowing that Ethan's spirit would forever dance in the petals that fell. In that moment, Sophie chose to honour their love, a love that would forever illuminate her journey, guiding her through the darkness into a dawn filled with endless possibilities.

With renewed strength, she stepped forward, carrying the echoes of their laughter in her heart, ready to write the next chapter of her life—one that would forever be intertwined with the eternal, beautiful bond they had shared.

AUTHOR'S MESSAGE AND CONCLUSION

If you're reading this page, I hope you've fully immersed yourself in the journey of Ethan and Sophie by reading all the chapters of 'A Sleeping Eight'. If you haven't finished the book yet, I encourage you to do so before reading this message.

Writing 'A Sleeping Eight' has been a journey into the depths of love, loss, and resilience. Through Sophie and Ethan's story, I wanted to show that love can transcend time and space—a bond that remains strong, even in the face of tragedy.

If there's one message I hope you take away from this book, it's this: please don't be like Paul. His choices remind us of how destructive jealousy and anger can be. Instead, strive for understanding, compassion, and love in your relationships. We have the power to create connections that uplift and inspire, rather than tear us apart.

As you finish this book, keep in mind that love is a lasting force. It's found in the shared moments, the laughter, and the little things that remind us of those we care about. Like A Sleeping Eight, love is infinite, looping back on itself and forever intertwined.

Thank you for joining me on this journey. I hope you find strength in your own stories and embrace the endless possibilities that love can bring. Love is a powerful force, and may it always guide you forward.

With gratitude,
-ROCHAK AGARWAL